# THE HUNGRY TOAD

by Janelle Cherrington
Illustrated by Horacio Elana

SCHOLASTIC

There was once a toad
named Toad.

2

Toad was always hungry.

He ate and ate and ate, but he

always wanted more.

Like most toads, he could puff
out his throat to croak. His throat
could get very, very big.

One day Toad ate and ate,

but he was still hungry.

Then he saw a bar of soap.

Gulp! It got stuck in his throat.

So Toad hopped down the
road to see the doctor.

"A toad does not eat soap,"
said the doctor as she took it out.

The next day Toad ate and ate,
but he was still hungry.

He saw a toaster. Gulp! It got
stuck in his throat.

The doctor said, "Toads do not eat toasters, and toads do not eat soap! I will make a list for you. Don't eat these things again!"

8

The next day Toad ate and ate,
but he was still hungry.

He went to the park. Gulp! Toad
ate a big foam football!

The doctor was mad.

"Give me your list," she said.

"I must add something to it!"

The next day Toad ate and ate,
but he was still hungry.

He met his friend. Gulp! Toad
ate her coat.

The doctor was very mad!
"What toad eats coats? No one
eats coats," she groaned.

The next day Toad ate and ate,

but he was still hungry.

He looked around. He saw a

rowboat. He checked his list.

"A boat is not on my list," he said. "Can I eat a boat?"

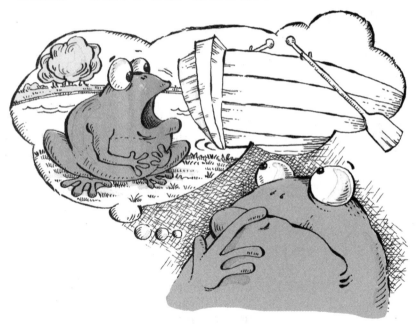

"Nope. I'd better not."

## My Words
*again
*better
*I'd
*park

## oa

| | |
|---|---|
| boat | road |
| coat | soap |
| croak | throat |
| foam | toad |
| groaned | |

**Story Words:** bar, doctor, football, toaster

**\*new high frequency words**

ISBN 0-590-99931-1     Copyright © 1997 by Scholastic Inc.     All rights reserved.     Printed in the U.S.A.